The
Wheels
on the
Bus

SO-AJI-385

To Alice Kovalski

88-375

Kids Can Press Ltd. gratefully
acknowledges the assistance of the
Canada Council and the Ontario Arts
Council in the production of this book.

**Canadian Cataloguing in
Publication Data**

Kovalski, Maryann.
   The wheels on the bus

ISBN 0-921103-09-3

I. Title.

PS8571.096W48
1987   jC813'.54   C87-093497-X
PZ7.K87Wh 1987

$10.95

Text and Illustrations Copyright © 1987
by Maryann Kovalski
Musical notation by Miriam Katzin

All rights reserved. No part of this
publication may be reproduced, stored in
a retrieval system, or transmitted in any
form or by any means, electronic,
mechanical photocopying, recording or
otherwise, without prior written
permission of

Kids Can Press Ltd.,
585½ Bloor Street West,
Toronto, Ontario, Canada, M6G 1K5.

Printed by Everbest Printing Co., Ltd.,
Hong Kong

10 9 8 7 6 5 4 3

Maryann Kovalski

The Wheels on the Bus

Kids Can Press Ltd.
Toronto

One day, Grandma took Jenny and Joanna shopping for new winter coats.

They tried on long coats and short coats, blue coats and red coats, plaid coats and even rain coats. Joanna chose a coat with wooden barrel buttons. Jenny liked it too, because of the hood.

When it was time to go home, the bus didn't come for a long time and everyone grew tired. "I have an idea, sweeties," said Grandma. "Let's sing a song my Granny sang with me when I was a little girl." And so they began to sing . . .

W. P. BATE SCHOOL

The   wheels on the   bus   go   round and

round   round and   round   round and

round. The   wheels on the   bus   go

round and   round   all

around the   town.

The wipers on the bus go swish, swish, swish
   swish, swish, swish
   swish, swish, swish
The wipers on the bus go swish, swish, swish
   all around the town.

The people on the bus hop on and off
   on and off
   on and off
The people on the bus hop on and off
   all around the town.

The horn on the bus goes toot, toot, toot
    toot, toot, toot
    toot, toot, toot
The horn on the bus goes toot, toot, toot
    all around the town.

The money on the bus goes clink, clink, clink
  clink, clink, clink
  clink, clink, clink
The money on the bus goes clink, clink, clink
  all around the town.

The people on the bus go up and down
   up and down
   up and down
The people on the bus go up and down
   all around the town.

The babies on the bus go waaa, waaa, waaa
   waaa, waaa, waaa
   waaa, waaa, waaa
The babies on the bus go waaa, waaa, waaa
   all around the town.

The parents on the bus go ssh, ssh, ssh
   ssh, ssh, ssh
   ssh, ssh, ssh
The parents on the bus go ssh, ssh, ssh
   all around the town.

The wheels on the bus go round and round
   round and round
   round and round
The wheels on the bus go round and round
   all around the town.

Grandma, Jenny and Joanna had so much fun singing
that . . .

They missed the bus!   So . . .

They took a taxi.

The end

W. P. BATE SCHOOL